"I'm so tired," yawned Mamma Duck,
"it's time for us day creatures to sleep."
"I'm coming," said Daisy.
"Sleep," said Pip.

But all around them,
night creatures played
in the twilight.
Mamma Duck
began to snore.

"Hello!" squeaked Twitch the mouse.
"Coo!" said Daisy.
"Pip!" went Pip

Twitch chased the moths as they fluttered around and around Mamma Duck. Daisy chased Twitch, and Pip chased Daisy.

flitter flutte

trop

trip

trip

trop

flutter flutter

swish swash

Through the flowers went the moths, Twitch, Daisy and Pip.

flutter

flitter

plop plip

Away and over the moonlit puddles.

In and out of the shadows,

went the moths, Twitch, Daisy and Pip.

But then a cloud covered the moon.
The moths flittered and fluttered
into the darkness, and so did Twitch.
Daisy and Pip stopped.

Everything was quiet and still.
"Coo, the moon's gone, it's
really dark!" said Daisy.
"Dark!" squeaked Pip.

"Where's Mamma?" squeaked Pip.
"I don't know, it's too dark, I can't
see!" said Daisy.

The shadows grew...

In the stillness, a twig snapped!
"Is that you, Twitch?" cried Daisy.

Something began to flap and flap!

Flap

Flap

"Help!" screamed Daisy.
"Mamma!" cried Pip.

"It's only Owl," said Twitch. "Follow me,
I'm a night creature; I can see."

So Daisy and Pip followed Twitch...

...out of the shadows,
over the puddles,

through the flowers,
and back to Mamma Duck...

...and under her soft, warm wing.

"Thanks, Twitch!"
said Daisy.

Mamma Duck snored.
"I'm tired and it's too dark
for us to play," said Daisy.
"Too dark," yawned Pip.

Twoo!
Hoo!
Hoo!

flitter flutter

The moon broke free of the clouds
and Twitch and the night creatures
played in the moonlight, whilst...

...the day creatures didn't.